Pirate Hank's Plank

by Penny Dolan and
Nacho Gomez

W
FRANKLIN WATTS
LONDON • SYDNEY

Franklin Watts

First published in Great Britain in 2016 by
The Watts Publishing Group

Series Editor: Jackie Hamley
Series Advisor: Catherine Glavina
Series Designer: Peter Scoulding

A CIP catalogue record for this book is available from the British Library.

ISBN 978 1 4451 4581 5 (hbk)
ISBN 978 1 4451 4579 2 (pbk)
ISBN 978 1 4451 4580 8 (library ebook)

Printed in China

Franklin Watts
An imprint of
Hachette Children's Group
Part of The Watts Publishing Group
Carmelite House
50 Victoria Embankment
London EC4Y 0DZ

An Hachette UK company.
www.hachette.co.uk

www.franklinwatts.co.uk

The sea was calm and
the sky was blue.

Suddenly, Joe heard a loud shout.

"Over there! A ship!" called Spy-Eye Sam.

At first, everyone was excited.

The strange ship drew closer and closer.

Then they saw the flag.

"It's a pirate ship!" shouted old Captain Cod-Face.

Too late! The band of pirates leaped aboard.

The crew feared for their lives.

The pirate chief boarded the ship. He walked around the deck, sword in hand.

“I am Hard-Nose Hank.
Beware this plank!”

Everyone looked at the plank, and at the deep, deep sea.

Nobody wanted to walk the plank.

"Who will go first?" asked Hank, smiling his mean pirate smile.

He put his boot on a big barrel. Nobody spoke.

Joe thought. He looked hard into Hank's eyes. "I will," he said, stepping forward.

"Now?" said Hank, grinning. "Really?"

"Yes. I've got a great idea," said Joe. "Just watch."

Joe put the plank across the barrel.

“Sit on that end,” he said, and Hard-Nose Hank did.

“This is great!” Hank shouted. “Thanks!”

They played see-saw for hours.

Then they played swinging from the rigging and all sorts of games ...

... until it was time to sail away again.

Puzzle 1

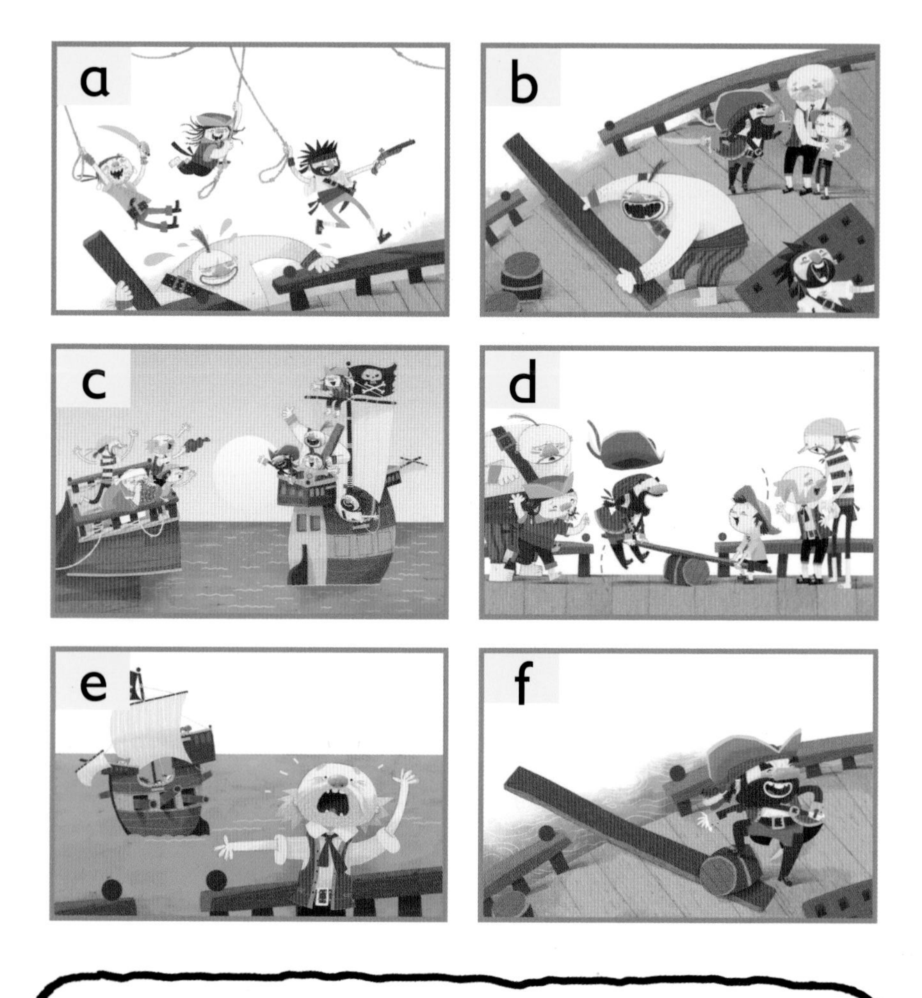

Put these pictures in the correct order.
Now tell the story in your own words.
Can you think of a different ending?

Puzzle 2

excited scared
terrified

happy thrilled
worried

Choose the words which best describe Captain Cod-Face at the beginning and end of the story. Can you think of any more?